ASHLEE TATE

The SLEEPOVER

by Michele Jakubowski

illustrated by Hédi Fekete

Curious Fox
a capstone company-publishers for children

Raintree is an imprint of Capstone Global Library Limited, a company incorporated in England and Wales having its registered office at 264 Banbury Road, Oxford, OX2 7DY – Registered company number: 6695582

www.raintree.co.uk
myorders@raintree.co.uk

Text © Capstone Global Library Limited 2017

The moral rights of the proprietor have been asserted.

Edited by Eliza Leahy and Helen Cox Cannons
Designed by Lori Bye
Original illustrations © Capstone 2016
Illustrated by Hédi Fekete
Production by Laura Manthe
Printed and bound in China

ISBN 978 1 4747 2042 7
20 19 18 17 16
10 9 8 7 6 5 4 3 2 1

British Library Cataloguing in Publication Data
A full catalogue record for this book is available from the British Library.

Acknowledgements
Every effort has been made to contact copyright holders of material reproduced in this book. Any omissions will be rectified in subsequent printings if notice is given to the publisher.

All the internet addresses (URLs) given in this book were valid at the time of going to press.
internet, some addresses may have changed, or
since publication. While the author and publisher
readers, no responsibility for any such changes
the author or the publisher.

contents

chapter one
Gymnastics. 7

chapter two
A perfect plan 14

chapter three
Games, games, games. 21

chapter four
Arts and crafts 29

chapter five
Change of plans. 38

chapter six
The party. 48

Ash

Ashley "Ash" Sanchez may be small, but she's mighty! Ash likes to play all types of games – from sport to video games – and she loves to win. Ash may be loud and silly, but more than anything, she is a great friend!

Lee

Ashlee Taylor, otherwise known as Lee, is tall and graceful. When Lee is not twirling around at her dance classes, she can be found drawing or painting. Lee may be shy around new people, but she is very kind!

chapter one

{ GYMNASTICS }

Best friends Ashley Sanchez and Ashlee Taylor had two things in common. They were both eight years old and they both loved their gymnastics class.

Apart from those two things, Ashley and Ashlee were different in almost every way. Ashley, or Ash as her friends called her, was small. Ashlee, otherwise known as Lee, was much taller.

Ashley Small and Ashlee Tall, as some of their friends called them, used to live in the same apartment building. Now Lee and her family had moved to a house a few streets away. After Lee moved, it was hard finding time to spend together. Both girls were busy. Ash loved to play sport. Lee adored her dance classes. After a while, they finally found an activity they both enjoyed – gymnastics.

One of the best things about their gymnastics class was the new friends they had made. As the class was starting, Ash and Lee ran to the mat to join Sophie and Prisha.

"Hello, everyone! I'm here!" Ash
called. She threw her arms into the air
and twirled around. All the girls giggled.
Ash loved attention. She also enjoyed
making people laugh.

Lee smiled and waved at her new friends. Although she was still a little shy around Sophie and Prisha, she was pleased to see them.

At the start of each class, everyone formed a big circle on the mat. Two of the instructors stood in the middle of the circle. They led the class through stretching and warm-ups.

As they bent over to touch their toes, the girls played a game they called "Make Me Laugh". The point of the game was to get the other girls to laugh out loud by making funny faces and noises. Sophie was usually the first one to laugh.

As Ash stretched, she made noises that sounded like a monkey. Sophie giggled. She looked away to keep from laughing harder. On her other side, Sophie found Lee upside down touching her toes. She was sticking out her tongue and crossing her eyes. That was too much for Sophie. She laughed so hard, she tumbled onto the mat. As the girls helped her up, they all burst out laughing.

When they finished their stretches, one of the instructors said, "Just a reminder, everybody. We have one class left. After next week there will be a four-week break before the next session."

"Only one more class?" Ash asked her friends sadly. "That means we won't see each other anymore!"

"We should make sure our parents sign us up for the next session," Lee said.

"Good idea!" said Prisha.

Ash was still not happy. "But we still have to wait four weeks to see each other!"

All four girls were sad now. They knew Ash was right. Four weeks was going to feel like forever!

chapter two

{ A PERFECT PLAN }

A few days after their gymnastics class, Ash and Lee got together at Ash's apartment. They were having a great time playing their favourite video game, Dance! Dance! Dance!

Ash loved video games! She had a huge collection. Her favourites were the ones where she could get up and play along.

Lee didn't really like video games. She watched Ash play sometimes, but after a while she usually got bored.

Dance! Dance! Dance! was the one video game they both enjoyed. As they danced along with the game, Ash and Lee each held a controller. They received points for following the dancers in the game correctly. As the song ended, their scores were displayed on the screen.

"You won again," Ash said.

"I did?" Lee asked. She had been having so much fun, she had forgotten about the points.

Ash did not like to lose. She pointed
her controller at the screen to start a new
game. "Let's try again. I think I made a
mistake where you spin around."

Lee put down her controller. "Can we eat our snack first?" she asked. "I need a break."

"Okay," Ash agreed. "But after that, let's play again."

As the girls sat on the sofa they realized how hungry and thirsty they were from all the dancing. They munched on some rice cakes and drank some juice.

Ash made a loud slurping noise as she finished her juice. "I'm still sad about gymnastics ending," she said. "I'm really going to miss Sophie and Prisha."

"It's not really ending," said Lee. "Sophie and Prisha are both going to sign up for the next session."

Ash frowned. "I know. But four weeks is a long time to go without seeing our new friends."

Now Lee was frowning too. "That's true."

Ash finished her juice and then put the carton on the table. She was quiet for a moment. Then she said, "Hey, I've got an idea!"

"What is it?" Lee asked.

"We could have a sleepover party with Sophie and Prisha!" Ash said excitedly.

"That's a great idea!" Lee said.

The girls took one look at each other and then raced to the kitchen where their mums were chatting.

Mrs Sanchez and Mrs Taylor both agreed that a sleepover was a wonderful idea. They decided to have the sleepover at Lee's house. They picked a date for two weeks after their last gymnastics class. Ash and Lee decided to make invitations and hand them out at the next class.

The girls were thrilled! They got started on making their invitations straight away.

chapter three

{ GAMES, GAMES, GAMES }

Ash and Lee couldn't wait for gymnastics class! As they entered the gym, they raced to find Sophie and Prisha to deliver their invitations.

"They are so pretty!" Sophie cried.

"I can't wait!" Prisha added.

The instructors called everyone to the big mat for stretching.

Instead of playing "Make Me Laugh" while they did their stretches, the girls talked about the sleepover.

"It was my idea," Ash told them as they did star jumps.

"Yes, but it will be at my house," Lee said quickly.

"It'll be so much fun," Prisha said.

"I'm so excited!" Sophie added.

After they stretched, the class divided into two groups. Ash and Lee were split up. They had never been in separate groups before, and they didn't like it.

"It's okay," Ash told Lee. "You're still with Sophie and I'm with Prisha."

Lee was unsure. Being with Ash always made her feel more comfortable.

"Come on! We get to do tumbling first!" Sophie said to Lee.

Lee loved tumbling. She waved goodbye to Ash and Prisha as she made her way to the tumbling mat.

Ash and Prisha went off to the balance beam. Ash liked the balance beam, but she always had to focus so that she wouldn't fall. At first, they had used a beam that was on the ground. It wasn't a disaster if she fell off that beam. Now the beam was higher off the ground. Ash was determined not to fall.

The instructor told the group to line up to take turns on the beam. As Ash and Prisha waited for their turns, they talked about the sleepover.

"I've got it all planned," Ash said.
"We are going to play games all night."

"I love games!" Prisha said. She
clapped her hands with excitement.
"What games are we going to play?"

"I've been making a list of ideas. I know that one of the games will be charades! It's my favourite and I'm really good at it. I've already started writing down clues," Ash told her.

"What else are we going to do?" Prisha asked.

Ash thought for a moment. "Well, we'll definitely eat some yummy snacks," she said. "Like popcorn."

"Yum!" Prisha smiled.

When it was Ash's turn on the balance beam she found it hard to concentrate.

She was thinking about the sleepover and how much fun they were going to have. Suddenly, Ash had a great idea! She could bring her video games, and they could have a video game tournament. Maybe there would even be a prize for the winner!

Ash was so busy thinking about her idea, she wasn't paying attention to the balance beam. She slipped and fell off. Thankfully, there was a mat underneath the beam, so she wasn't hurt.

When Prisha finished her turn on the beam, she joined Ash at the back of the line.

"Are you okay?" Prisha asked. "I saw you fall off the beam."

"I'm fine," Ash told her. She was frustrated with herself for not doing well.

"I keep thinking about the sleepover party," Prisha said. "It's going to be so much fun!"

Ash remembered her video game idea for the party. It made her feel much better.

"It definitely is! I've had another great idea, but I want to make it a surprise," Ash said with a smile. "This is going to be the best sleepover ever!"

chapter four

{ ARTS AND CRAFTS }

Lee felt nervous as she went to the
tumbling mat with Sophie. She really
liked tumbling and she really liked
Sophie, but she felt nervous trying new
things without Ash.

"Tumbling is my favourite gymnastics
activity," Sophie told Lee.

Lee smiled and nodded her head. She
felt very shy.

"What are we going to do at the sleepover?" Sophie asked.

"Um," Lee began. She wished Ash was in their group. Maybe then she wouldn't feel so shy.

Just then, the instructor clapped her hands to get everyone's attention. "Can you believe it?" she said. "Today is our last class. I think we're ready to work on some more difficult tumbling moves!"

The group cheered.

"Lee, would you please come up to the front?" the instructor asked. "I've seen how well you tumble. I'd like you to show the class what we'll be doing."

Lee froze. Suddenly her body felt very heavy. She couldn't move.

"Go ahead. You're a great tumbler," Sophie whispered.

This made Lee feel better, but she was still very nervous. She felt shaky as she walked to the front of the mat.

"Have you ever done a back walkover?" the instructor asked.

Lee nodded. She had learned a lot of tumbling moves at her dance classes.

"Great!" the instructor said. "Class, Lee is going to show us how to do a back walkover."

Lee took a deep breath. With the instructor close by for help, Lee did a back walkover. When she had finished, the girls cheered for her.

Lee opened her eyes and saw everyone smiling at her. She had done it!

Lee went back to her place on the mat. Sophie gave her a high-five and said, "Well done!"

As they lined up to practise their walkovers, Lee felt great. She couldn't believe she'd gone in front of the group!

"What do you think we'll do at the sleepover?" Sophie asked Lee.

"I was thinking we could do arts and crafts," Lee said softly.

"Sounds fun," Sophie said. "What will we make?"

Lee was happy that Sophie liked her idea. "I've got a lot of craft materials. We can set up an art studio in the basement," she said.

"Great!" Sophie smiled.

"We can have a paint station and a place to make friendship bracelets," Lee said. "I also have a new origami book that will show us how to make paper animals."

Sophie and Lee had reached the front of the line. It was Sophie's turn to try a back walkover.

"Good luck!" Lee said.

While Sophie worked with the instructor on her back walkover, Lee had another great idea for the sleepover. They could make hand puppets and put on a show! It would be so much fun!

When Sophie had done her back walkover, Lee continued talking about the sleepover.

"I've even been planning our snacks, too," Lee said. "We can melt some chocolate and dip strawberries, marshmallows and biscuits in it. Maybe we can even decorate cupcakes!"

"That sounds delicious," Sophie said.

"Yep." Lee smiled and nodded. "This is going to be the best sleepover ever!"

chapter five

{ CHANGE OF PLANS }

The sleepover was less than a week away. Ash and Lee had planned to spend the afternoon at Lee's house getting ready for the party.

Lee was waiting for Ash at the front door when she arrived. Ash was carrying a big bag that looked very heavy. She stumbled as she climbed the front steps.

"What's in the bag?" Lee asked.

"Stuff for the party," Ash said. "Let's go up to your room and I'll show you."

Once upstairs, Ash noticed a large square object in the middle of Lee's room. It had a blanket covering it.

Ash put down her bag with a huff. "What's that?" she asked, pointing to the blanket.

A huge smile crossed Lee's face. "It's for the party," she said.

Ash was confused. "What is it?"

"I couldn't wait to tell you," Lee began. "I've been making plans for the sleepover! Sophie and I talked about it. I decided that our sleepover will have an arts and crafts theme, and we'll make lots of things. We're also going to have a chocolate bar and we'll decorate our own cupcakes. It's going to be really fun!"

Lee clasped her hands together and waited for Ash's response. She was surprised when Ash said simply, "No, we're not doing any of that."

"We're not?" Lee asked. "Why not?"

Ash began pulling things out of her bag. "Because I already told Prisha that we're going to have a game night. I know you're not a big fan of video games, so I brought some along for practice."

The smile left Lee's face as she watched Ash pull video games out of her bag. Then Ash pulled out a rolled up piece of poster board.

"I decided to make it a tournament," Ash said as she unrolled the poster board. She had divided the board into four squares. At the top of each square she had written their names.

"We're going to keep track of who wins each game on this board. Whoever wins the most will get a prize!" Ash told her. "We'll probably be too busy to decorate cupcakes. It will be easier if we just snack on popcorn and crisps instead."

Lee didn't like to argue. She also didn't like the fact that Ash thought her own plans were better.

"I suppose we can play some games," Lee mumbled. "As long as we have time for the puppet show."

"The what?" Ash asked.

Lee pulled the blanket off of the object on the floor. Underneath was a big box Lee had turned into a stage.

Welcome to our show!

She had cut out a hole on one side and painted "Welcome to our show!" over the top. She had even glued felt curtains on the sides. It looked fantastic!

"That's really cool!" Ash said. "But we probably won't have time."

"But I've already told Sophie," Lee said. She was starting to feel angry. "She's really excited about doing arts and crafts."

"Well, I already told Prisha about playing games, and that's what she wants to do," Ash said as she folded her arms.

She was beginning to get angry that Lee was trying to change her plans. She didn't want to fight, but she had been so excited.

Both girls were frustrated and unsure of what to do next. Neither of them wanted to give up their plans.

As they stood in silence, they both had the same thought: *This is going to be the worst sleepover ever!*

chapter six

{ THE PARTY }

The night of the sleepover was finally here! Sophie, Prisha and Ash arrived at Lee's house and made their way down to the playroom in the basement.

"Hooray! Sleepover time!" Sophie said. She gave each girl a big hug.

"Woo-hoo!" Prisha added. "It feels like so long since I've seen you all, and it's only been two weeks."

Ash and Lee smiled but didn't say anything. They hadn't seen each other since their argument at Lee's house the week before. Neither of them had agreed to give up their plans. They both worried that the party was going to be a disaster.

"What game are we going to play first?" Prisha asked.

"Game?" Sophie was confused. "I thought we were going to paint first and then do some craft?"

"Actually, we're going to play a game first," Lee said quietly.

Ash looked up in surprise. "We are?"

"Yep. It's called Guess the Sketch," Lee said. She brought over her whiteboard. "It's like charades, but you have to draw the clues for your partner instead of acting them out. It's like a game and art at the same time."

Ash smiled at Lee. She was so grateful that her friend had found something they would both want to do.

Suddenly Ash remembered something. She jumped up and went towards the stairs. "I'll be right back," she said.

Prisha, Sophie and Lee were writing down clues on slips of paper when Ash returned. She was carrying two large containers.

"I brought some snacks we can eat while we're playing," Ash told them.

"Yum!" Prisha said.

"My mum and I made some sweet and salty popcorn. We also made these biscuits," Ash said.

"Chocolate! My absolute favourite food," Lee said.

"I know." Ash smiled.

Lee gave Ash a hug and said, "I'm glad we found things we both like for the party."

"Me too," Ash replied.

The girls had so much fun playing Lee's game. They giggled and laughed at the silly drawings and funny answers they shouted.

When they had played all of the clues, Prisha asked, "What game are we going to play next?"

"I was thinking we could put on a puppet show," Ash said, looking at Lee and smiling.

Lee smiled back. "Yes, and after that we can play some more games."

"This is the best sleepover ever!" Sophie said, and they all agreed.

GLOSSARY

argument disagreement or a discussion in which people express differing opinions

charades game in which players try to guess a word or phrase from another person acting out clues

deliver take something to someone

disaster outcome in which everything goes wrong

grateful thankful

invitation written or spoken request for someone to go somewhere or do something

session period of time devoted to a certain activity

slurp drink or eat something noisily

stretch straighten your body, your arms or your legs to get your muscles ready for exercise

tournament series of games or contests in which a number of people compete for a championship or prize

tumbler someone who performs acrobatic movements such as somersaults or cartwheels

walkover gymnastic move in which the gymnast moves from a standing position, through a handstand position and back to a standing position while "walking" her feet through the air

TALK ABOUT IT

1. When Ash and Lee discover they won't see their new friends Prisha and Sophie at gymnastics for four weeks, they're upset. Discuss how they came up with a solution to their problem. What are some other solutions they could have tried?

2. Ash would like to play games all night at the sleepover party. Lee prefers an arts and crafts theme. Eventually they come up with Guess the Sketch as an activity that includes both. Can you think of some other activities that would combine Ash and Lee's interests? Talk about the possibilities.

3. Do you think Ash and Lee's sleepover party was a success? Discuss why or why not.

WRITE IT DOWN

1. Ash and Lee have a disagreement about their sleepover party. Write a paragraph explaining what the disagreement was and how they worked it out, using examples from the text.

2. If Ash had only agreed to play games and Lee had only agreed to do crafts, what would their sleepover party have been like? Imagine this happened, and write a scene from the sleepover.

3. Plan your own sleepover party! Write lists of the games you would play, crafts you'd complete, food you'd eat, films you would watch and the guests you would invite.

HOW TO MAKE INVITATIONS

Making invitations is the first step to planning any party – just ask Ash and Lee! Invitations give you the chance to send out information about your event. They can also be a good opportunity to show off what your event is all about! For instance, if you're having a spa-themed sleepover party, your invitations might include doodles of nail polish bottles, bubbles or sleeping bags. If you're having a sport-themed barbecue, your invitations might show drawings of burgers, fries, footballs or Frisbees.

what you need

- coloured pencils or felt-tip pens
- stickers
- glitter
- paper

what you do

There's no step-by-step formula for making invitations. Make sure you include important information, such as the time and date of your event. Also let your friends know if there is anything specific they should bring. If you want to, you can include information about what you'll be doing and eating at the party, so your friends know what to expect. Make sure you end your invitation by asking your friends to RSVP. Once you have responses, you'll know just how much food and space you'll need for your event!

ABOUT THE AUTHOR

Michele Jakubowski has the teachers in her life to thank for her love of reading and writing. While writing has always been a passion for Michele, she believes it is the books she has read throughout the years, and the teachers who recommended them, that have made her the storyteller she is today. Michele lives in Ohio, USA, with her husband, John, and their children, Jack and Mia.

ABOUT THE ILLUSTRATOR

Born in Transylvania, Hédi Fekete grew up watching and drawing her favourite cartoon characters. Each night, her mother read her beautiful bedtime stories, which made her love for storytelling grow. Hédi's love for books and animation stuck with her through the years, inspiring her to become an illustrator, digital artist and animator.

MAKE SURE TO CHECK OUT ALL THE TITLES IN THE ASHLEY SMALL AND ASHLEE TALL SERIES!

BEST FRIENDS FOREVER?

BRUSHES AND BASKETBALLS

THE GRASS IS ALWAYS GREENER

THE SLEEPOVER